Introduction

Sheep and Ireland go together like a woolly jumper and a chilly day. Our fuzzy friends have been on the island for almost as long as humans have, and there are actually more of them than us!

Not only will you spot them grazing happily in verdant valleys, rambling on hills and causing traffic chaos on country roads, you'll also notice the number of placenames dedicated to our ovine compatriots: Sheep's Head in Cork, Lamb's Rock in Kerry, Sheephaven in Donegal, Glenageary (Valley of the Sheep) in Dublin, Ram Head in Waterford ... and Lamb Islands all over the place. 'Tis no surprise that the wonderful woollie is our unofficial national symbol.

In this book, we bring you a pure celebration of the Irish sheep. Let's put aside talk of sustainability and a struggling wool industry and instead rejoice in our lovely lambs, beautiful Blackfaces and stunning Suffolks. As the Irish proverb goes, 'There never was a scabby sheep in a flock that didn't like to have a comrade.' Love is love.

Life on the edge: Sheep on Fanad Head Peninsula in County Donegal, with Fanad Lighthouse in the background.

Above: May the fleece be with you! A flock basking in the summer sunshine on the Dingle Peninsula, County Kerry, with the otherworldly Skellig Islands in the background.

Opposite: Lamb triplets huddle in the shelter of a traditional stone wall in County Leitrim.

Opposite: A Donegal Blackface has a wee think.

Above: Sheep grazing in front of the Rock of Cashel, an iconic cluster of medieval buildings in County Tipperary that was once the seat of the Kings of Munster.

A Blackface ewe enjoying a gorgeous sunset at the Gap of Dunloe, which separates the MacGillycuddy's Reeks from the Purple Mountains near Killarney in County Kerry.

Above: Big coat weather! A snowy day by Benbulben in County Sligo.

Opposite: Baby lambs stay close to their mums in Mount Temple, County Westmeath.

Opposite: Trying out the old camouflage in Connemara, Galway.

Below: The aptly named Sheep's Head Peninsula in County Cork.

Pondering the coming winter in *Game of Thrones* territory, Ballintoy, County Antrim.

It's lonely at the top! Solo travellers in the Mountains of Mourne, County Down (**above**); on sacred Croagh Patrick in County Mayo (**opposite, top**); and in the Comeraghs in County Waterford (**opposite, bottom**).

A Cheviot stands out against the purple heather high in the Wicklow Mountains.

Along with the Cheviot, the most common breeds found in Ireland are (**clockwise from above**): the Scottish Blackface, the Texel and the Suffolk.

A beautiful sunrise on the Ring of Kerry, with Valentia Island in the distance.

Above: It's pasture bedtime! Enjoying a snuggle with mum in a Kerry meadow.

Opposite: A lovely little lamb on Sheep's Head Way in West Cork.

In some breeds of Irish sheep, both males and females have horns; in others, just the males; and in others, neither – these are called 'polled' sheep. Some unusual fellows, like our friend here, have an amazing *four* horns. Bound to impress the ladies!

A border collie rounding up his flock at the Kissane Sheep Farm in Kenmare, County Kerry.

May the road rise up to meet you: Tackling the commute on Irish highways and byways.

All sheeps and sizes can enjoy this glorious mountain landscape in Gleninchaquin Park in Kerry.

Which way's the beach? These lucky woollies watch the wild Atlantic waves over Ballymastocker Bay, County Donegal.

Hanging out by the passage tombs at Dowth (**left**) and Newgrange (**above**) in County Meath, which date back some five thousand years. Farming in Ireland goes back even further: the first sheep, cows, pigs and goats were domesticated around 4000BC.

Traditional hand or blade shearing is still carried out in some parts of Ireland, especially by farmers with small flocks. Meanwhile, all around the country, Irish woollen mills transform these fleeces into gorgeous textiles and clothing, famous the world over.

The evening sun over the cliffs at Slieve League, Donegal.

Man's best friends:

A Mayo famer and his pups take the flock home.

Trying to figure out the road signs in rural Ireland. It's a head-scratcher!

Opposite: An Achill Blackface gives us the woolly eyeball.

Above: Shear up, everyone! Enjoying the sun on Inishbofin.

The end of another day
near Roundstone in County
Galway.

Out standing in his own (Sligo) field: Irish sheep are daubed with paint to help farmers identify their own, especially when flocks are free to wander on rolling hills. They're also marked during mating or 'tupping' season to show which rams and ewes have ... become acquainted!

Left: A sunny snooze on the Dingle Peninsula.

Above: Proud to be the black sheep of the family!

Dry stone walls, built without mortar, have been keeping sheep in (and the elements out) for millennia. It is estimated that there are around four hundred thousand kilometres of stone wall criss-crossing Ireland, mainly in the south and west.

Anois teacht an Earraigh: And now comes the Spring!